W9-ATJ-028

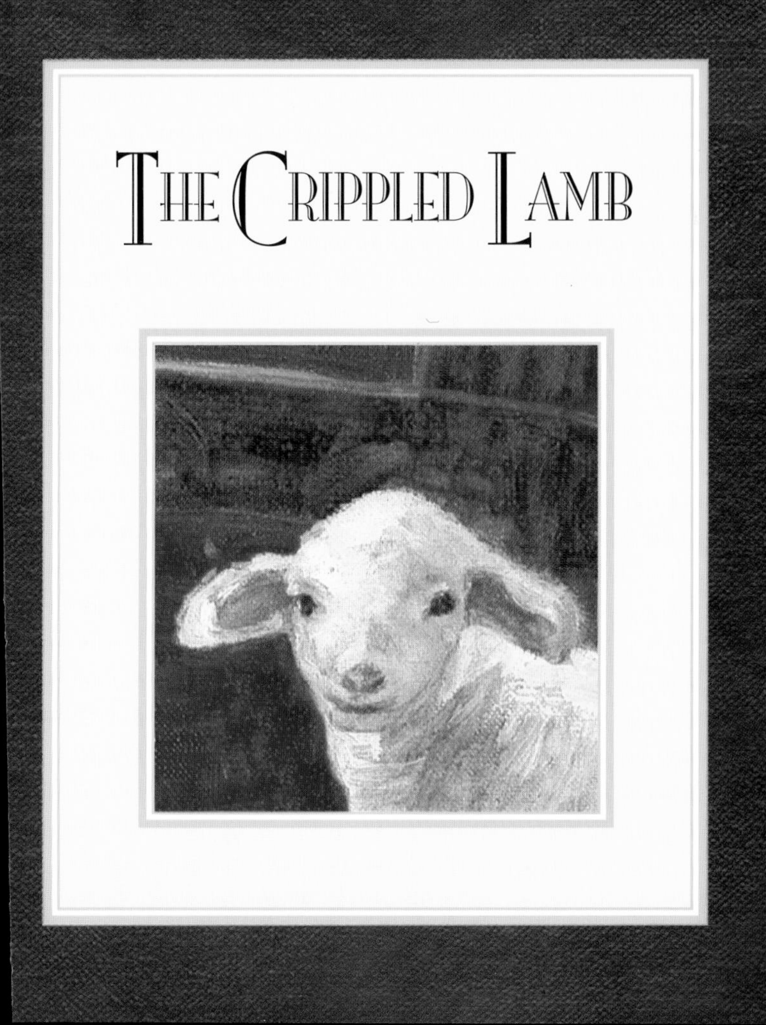
THE CRIPPLED LAMB

To our special friends—-
Kelly, Kasey, and Kara Wilson

Published in Nashville, Tennessee, by Tommy Nelson®, a Division of Thomas Nelson, Inc.

Library of Congress Cataloging-in-Publication Data

Lucado, Max.
The crippled lamb / by Max Lucado with Jenna, Andrea & Sara Lucado; illustrations by Liz Bonham.
p. cm.
Summary: A lamb who has always felt different and sad because of his black spots and his limp, feels his true worth when he is called upon to help keep the baby Jesus warm.
ISBN 0-8499-1005-6 (original hardcover)
ISBN 0-8499-7502-6 (board book)
ISBN 1-4003-0131-9 (4½ x 5½)
ISBN 1-4003-0007-X (box set)
[1. Sheep—Fiction. 2. Jesus Christ—-Nativity—Fiction.]
I. Bonham, Liz, ill. II. Title.
PZ7.L9684Cr 1994
[E]—dc20 94-19865
CIP
AC

Printed in China

02 03 04 05 LEO 5 4 3 2 1

THE CRIPPLED LAMB

by Max Lucado

with Jenna, Andrea & Sara Lucado

illustrated by Liz Bonham

www.tommynelson.com

A Division of Thomas Nelson, Inc.
www.ThomasNelson.com

Once upon a time there lived a little lamb named Joshua. He was white with black spots, black feet, and . . . sad eyes. Josh felt sad when he saw the other lambs running and jumping, because he couldn't.

Josh had been born with one leg that didn't work right. He always limped when he walked.

When he watched the other lambs run and play, Josh felt sad and alone—except when Abigail was around. Abigail was Josh's best friend. She was an old cow, and her voice was always kind and friendly.

Some of Josh's favorite hours were spent with Abigail.

She would spend hours with Josh, telling him stories. When Josh got sad because he could not run and jump and play in the grass, Abigail would say, "Don't be sad, little Joshua. God has a special place for those who feel left out."

Josh wanted to believe her. But it was hard. Some days he just felt alone.

Then one day the shepherds decided to take the lambs to the next valley where there was more grass. All the sheep were excited.

Josh hobbled over and took his place on the edge of the group, but the others started laughing at him.

"Go back, Slowpoke. We'll never get there if we have to wait on you!"

"Go back, Joshua."

Then he heard the shepherd's voice, "They are right, little Joshua. You better go back. This trip is too long for you. Go and spend the night in the stable."

Joshua turned slowly and began limping away.

Never before had Joshua felt so left out. A big tear slipped out of his eye, rolled down his nose, and fell on a rock.

"Don't be sad, little Joshua," said Abigail. "God has a special place for those who feel left out." The two friends walked to the stable together.

After eating some hay, Joshua lay down on some straw and closed his eyes. Abigail came and rested beside him. Josh was glad to have Abigail as a friend.

Soon Josh was asleep. He dreamed of running and jumping just like the other sheep. He dreamed of being in a place where he never felt left out.

Suddenly, strange noises woke him up.

"Abigail," he whispered, "wake up. I'm scared. Somebody is in here."

They looked across the dimly lighted stable. Josh and Abigail were surprised to see a baby lying on some fresh hay in the feed box. The baby's mother was resting on a big pile of hay beside the feed box.

Josh limped across the stable. He stopped next to the mother and looked into the baby's face. The baby was crying. He was cold. The woman picked up the baby and put him on the hay next to her.

Josh looked around for something to keep the baby warm.

Then Josh remembered his own soft, warm wool. Timidly, he walked over and curled up close to the baby.

"Thank you, little lamb," the baby's mother said softly.

Soon the little child stopped crying. About that time, a man entered the stable carrying some rags to cover the baby. "Look, Joseph, this little lamb has kept the new king warm."

A king? Joshua wondered who the baby might be.

"The baby's name is Jesus. He is God's Son. He came from heaven to teach us about God," the mother said.

Just then there was another noise at the door. It was the shepherds—the ones who had left Joshua behind.

"We saw a bright light and heard the angels . . ." they began. Then they saw Joshua next to the baby. "Joshua! Do you know who this baby is?"

The young mother smiled. "God has heard your prayer, little lamb. This baby is the answer."

Somehow Joshua knew this was a special child, and this was a special moment.

He also understood why he had been born with a crippled leg. Had he been like the other sheep, he would have been away in the valley. But since he was different, he was in the stable, among the first to welcome Jesus into the world.

Joshua turned and walked back to Abigail and took his place beside his friend. "You were right," he told her. "God does have a special place for me."